FIVE GOLD-SMUGGLING RINGS

DIANE KELLY

Copyright © 2023 Diane Kelly. Previously published by Amazon Publishing. All Rights Reserved

No part of this book may be reproduced, downloaded, transmitted, decompiled, reverse engineered, stored in, or introduced to any information storage and retrieval system, in any form, whether electronic or mechanical, without the author's prior written permission. Scanning, uploading, or distribution of this book via the Internet or any other means without permission is prohibited. Federal law requires that consumers purchase only authorized electronic versions and provides for criminal and civil penalties for producing or possessing pirated copies.

This book is a work of fiction. Names, characters, organizations, places, events, and incidents are either used fictitiously or products of the author's imagination. Any resemblance to actual persons, living or dead, or actual events is entirely coincidental.

❀ Created with Vellum

BOOKS BY DIANE KELLY

THE BUSTED SERIES:
Busted
Another Big Bust
Busting Out

THE MOUNTAIN LODGE MYSTERIES:
Getaway With Murder
A Trip With Trouble
Snow Place for Murder

THE SOUTHERN HOMEBREW SERIES:
The Moonshine Shack Murder
The Proof is in the Poison
Fiddling With Fate

THE HOUSE FLIPPER SERIES:
Dead as a Door Knocker
Dead in the Doorway
Murder With a View
Batten Down the Belfry

Primer and Punishment
Four-Alarm Homicide

THE PAW ENFORCEMENT SERIES:
Paw Enforcement
Paw and Order
Upholding the Paw (a bonus novella)
Laying Down the Paw
Against the Paw
Above the Paw
Enforcing the Paw
The Long Paw of the Law
Paw of the Jungle
Bending the Paw

THE TARA HOLLOWAY DEATH & TAXES SERIES:
Death, Taxes, and a French Manicure
Death, Taxes, and a Skinny No-Whip Latte
Death, Taxes, and Extra-Hold Hairspray
Death, Taxes, and a Sequined Clutch (a bonus novella)
Death, Taxes, and Peach Sangria
Death, Taxes, and Hot Pink Leg Warmers
Death, Taxes, and Green Tea Ice Cream
Death, Taxes, and Mistletoe Mayhem (a bonus novella)
Death, Taxes, and Silver Spurs
Death, Taxes, and Cheap Sunglasses
Death, Taxes, and a Chocolate Cannoli
Death, Taxes, and a Satin Garter
Death, Taxes, and Sweet Potato Fries
Death, Taxes, and Pecan Pie (a bonus novella)
Death, Taxes, and a Shotgun Wedding

OTHER MYSTERIES AND ROMANCES:
The Trouble with Digging Too Deep
Almost an Angel

Five Gold-Smuggling Rings
Love Unleashed
Love, Luck, and Little Green Men
One Magical Night
A Sappy Love Story

CHAPTER 1
A CASE FOR CHRISTMAS

I arrived at the Dallas Immigrations and Customs Enforcement office promptly at 9:03 Monday morning. Problem was, the weekly office-wide meeting began at 9:00. Guess I shouldn't have stayed up late watching *The Great British Baking Show* marathon.

After ditching my purse in my office and grabbing the flyers for the holiday party I'd coordinated, I sneaked in the door of the crowded conference room. My boss, Vince Beldaccio, narrowed his eyes at me in censure but continued speaking.

"Remember, folks," Beldaccio barked, "Christmas Eve is not a federal holiday. If you want the day off, you have to put in for vacation."

Uncle Sam could be such a party pooper.

As our boss updated the group on pending cases, I took a place along the back wall next to Agent Javier Carrasco. My coworker turned his gaze on me and damned if I didn't feel like a willing strawberry being dipped in the fondue of his molten-chocolate eyes. *Yummm . . .*

Agent Carrasco, or "Rasco" as he was known about the office, was a tough agent, with five years under his belt. He was as tall as me, his frame trimmed with lean muscle. His dark hair was slicked back with gel. He wore faded jeans, black biker boots, and a black leather jacket with more studs than the all-male revue at Chippendale's. Rasco's specialty was intercepting narcotics making their way up from Mexico. Thus, the badass outfit. He'd transferred to the Dallas office from Tucson two months ago.

When Beldaccio had first introduced Javier at a staff meeting, every female in the room exploded in a simultaneous orgasm. As I'd since learned though, while Rasco had sex appeal out the wazoo, his personality could use an upgrade. He was gruff, stingy with his words, impenetrable. A loner obsessed with his job.

The polar opposite of Rasco would be me. I was the office sweetheart, the beloved coworker who brought donuts on Fridays, remembered everyone's birthday with a card and balloons, and was always willing to help others with grunt work. While I'd never seen Rasco crack a smile, I wore a perpetual grin. You might think that odd for a federal agent, but once I'd hit 6'1" and 160 pounds at the age of fourteen, I realized that if I didn't smile I scared people, like some type of big-boned, blond-haired she-monster. Needless to say, my adolescence left something to be desired.

After a few more minutes of yammering about agents filing late reports (*guilty*), running personal errands while on duty (*guilty, but it was an emergency stop for a half-price purse sale*), and misusing our government computers to watch silly cat videos on YouTube (*guilty times ten—those cats are a riot!*), our boss asked if there were any questions. My hand shot into the air like an eager schoolgirl with the right answer to a history question. *The War of 1812!*

Beldaccio lifted his chin to indicate me. "Agent Dietrich?"

I scurried to the front of the room and waved the flyers like a cheerleader shaking her pom-poms. "Don't forget the holiday party a week from Friday!"

I handed stacks of flyers to the people on the front row so they could pass them back to the others. The flyers read:

Whether it's dreidels, candles, or mistletoe,
Hanukah, Kwanzaa, or Christmas,
Don't miss the ICE holiday party!!!
5:30 Friday, December 21st at the Ginger Man!!!
Bring your holiday spirit
and a white elephant gift!!!

I'd gone overboard with the exclamation points, but who could blame me? This was the most wonderful time of the year. Presents, sugar cookies, more presents, pumpkin pie, more presents . . . What's not to like?

When my flyers had made their way around the room, with Rasco passing them along but not taking one himself (*Grinch!*), Beldaccio wrapped things up with a clap of his hands. "Back to work, folks. Criminals don't arrest themselves."

Such wisdom and eloquence. Easy to see why he's in charge, huh?

My coworkers and I filed out of the room, turning right or left depending on the location of our digs. My office was at the end of the hall to the left, just before the supply closet and across from the restrooms. I spent my days listening to toilets flush and people rustling around for sticky notes or paper clips. Such is the life of a rookie.

I'd been with ICE six months. Before joining the feds, I'd spent five years as a civil investigator for the Texas Attorney General's Consumer Protection Department. My experience at the state level taught me how to dig for clues, conduct interviews, and peck away at a suspect's defense until it crumbled into dust. But I'd eventually learned all I could, and I wanted to take my career a step further. Also, I wanted a shiny badge and a gun. What girl doesn't yearn for a little bling? Especially bling that goes *bang!*

I was still in training at ICE, assisting other agents with their caseloads. With any luck, someday soon Beldaccio would deem me ready for a case of my own. It didn't have to be a big one. A little one against an elderly Chinese grandmother who smuggled Louis Vuitton knockoffs in from Shanghai would suffice. Just something I could call my own, call the shots on, and take credit for. *Nothing wrong with a little ambition, right?*

Back in my office, I plopped down in my chair, logged onto my computer, and pulled up my e-mail. Three new messages awaited me.

At the top of my inbox was an e-mail from Beldaccio's secretary, Nancy, reminding me to turn in my report on a recent news-making bust of an Indonesian man importing counterfeit Levi's jeans. *Paperwork. Uck.* Writing reports was the least interesting part of our jobs. It was far more fun to be out in the field, performing surveillance, questioning suspects, or executing an arrest.

That particular bust had been a blast. The agency had received a tip the target was selling fake jeans at Dallas Market Hall. Beldaccio assigned me to assist a male agent with the investigation. When we approached the suspect, he took off running, grabbing a fire extinguisher from the wall and spraying it at us. My coworker lost his footing in the foam, but I managed to wrangle the device from the suspect and turn the improvised weapon on him. By the time I was done the guy looked like a frosted wedding cake. Several people caught the takedown on their cell phones and shared it online and with the news media, who'd featured the footage on the six o'clock news. My fifteen minutes of fame.

The second e-mail was from a fellow agent asking for a file I'd been reviewing. *Hmm.* I dug through the pile on my desk.

Ah. There it is. I attached a routing slip and stuck the file in my outbox for the mail clerk.

I turned back to my computer, puzzled. I didn't recognize the sender of the third e-mail. The address sounded like one a mail-order bride might use. Kinshasa-cutie@gmail.com.

Whuh . . . ?

Knowing the server would've screened out infected communications, I opened the message.

Agent Angelika Dietrich,

I must speak with you. Meet me in the downtown Neiman Marcus evening wear department dressing room tomorrow at 2:30.

Sincerely,

A Woman Who Wants to Do Right

Again, *Whuh?*

I had no idea what to make of the message. It could be a ruse, sent by someone I'd taken down in a previous case. I'd made fools of more than one suspect who'd attempted to flee only to find himself tackled and restrained by yours truly. Not to brag, but I hadn't been the state high school shot put and pole vault champ three years in a row for nothing. Maybe the sender of the e-mail was leading me into a trap. But who would plan an ambush at Neiman's? It was too much for me to wrap my mind around.

I printed out a copy of the message and headed to my boss's office. I stopped in the doorway when I realized Beldaccio wasn't alone. He leaned back in his chair with his arms folded across his chest in his heavy-thinking pose. He waved me into the room.

Rasco sat in a wing chair, leaning forward, his face pensive. He glanced my way, irritation flickering across his face before he turned back to our boss. "Guerra's nervous. He plans to move the entire operation, including his stash."

"When is this going down?" Beldaccio asked.

6 DIANE KELLY

"Tomorrow evening," Rasco replied in his smooth-as-satin, Spanish-tinged voice.

Beldaccio exhaled sharply. "Take plenty of ammo and watch your back." My boss turned his attention to me now. "Whaddya need, Dietrich?"

I handed him the paper. "I received this strange e-mail this morning."

He read it over. "Any idea who this 'Kinshasa Cutie' is?"

"None."

Rasco looked from me to our boss. "Kinshasa's the capital of the DRC."

"DRC?" I wasn't familiar with the abbreviation.

"The Democratic Republic of the Congo," Rasco clarified.

I should've paid more attention in high school geography.

Beldaccio rubbed his chin before handing the printout to Rasco. "What do you make of this?"

Rasco read it over. "Unclear. It could be an informant stepping forward. Or it could be someone trying to snare Agent Dietrich."

Beldaccio looked up as if juggling the ideas in his head before turning his eyes back to Rasco. "You've got good instincts. What should we do?"

"I'd send her in," Rasco said, "but with cover."

Beldaccio nodded. "Why don't you go with her? You could teach her a thing or two."

Oh, I bet he could teach me all kinds of things, many of which would have nothing to do with our jobs as ICE agents. My body temperature soared at the thought.

Evidently Rasco was less excited about the prospect of teaming up with me than I was about teaming up with him. He frowned. "Babysitting a rookie? You sure that's the best use of my time?"

Babysitting? This guy better watch it or he'd find me ripping off his balls and shot-putting them down the hallway. I might be a rookie, but I was a damn good agent. Hard working. Smart. Fearless. Well, relatively fearless. That suspect with the shaved head and the teardrop tattoo beneath his eye had nearly made me wet myself, but other than that my undies had remained perfectly dry.

"She needs some training," Beldaccio replied. "You're one of the agency's top operatives. Who better to teach her the ropes?"

His ego assuaged, Rasco glanced my way. "Come to my office tomorrow at one." He skewered me with his gaze. "Don't be late."

Emotions battled in me as I walked back to my office. On one hand, I was excited an intriguing and possibly dangerous mission loomed on the horizon. I lived for action. On the other hand, Rasco was proving to be an absolute ass. Had I really thought his eyes looked like melted chocolate earlier? Nah. They were just everyday brown. Like an old shoe or cow manure.

At least this could be the start of a new case, one that might be mine to manage. I couldn't think of a better Christmas present than an investigation of my own.

CHAPTER 2
A CHINK IN THE ARMOR

I spent Tuesday morning helping a coworker inventory a cache of illegally imported pharmaceuticals he'd seized at a local drugstore. The majority of the drugs were hair growth pills. The remainder were anti-depressants. I had a feeling many were utilized by the same patients—men who were balding and moping about it. My opinion on the subject? *Man up!* Bald is sexy. Just look at Bruce Willis, Vin Diesel, and Dwayne "The Rock" Johnson. Each of them hairless, each of them hot. I'd do any of them in a heartbeat. Just don't tell Santa. He'd put me on his naughty list.

At 1:00 that afternoon, I headed to Agent Carrasco's office, eyeing the time on my phone and slowing my pace so I purposely arrived one minute late. That would teach the egomaniac to boss me around. Or maybe it just proved my immaturity.

Javier sat at his desk, the boots, jeans, and leather jacket gone today, replaced by shiny loafers, slacks, a white dress shirt, and a silk tie in a diamond-shaped print. This guy really knew how to dress. Most likely he'd received special attention from a lust-crazed saleswoman—or salesman.

I tapped my knuckles on his open door. "Ready to go, partner?"

He looked up at me, then immediately checked his watch. I fought the urge to snort.

"Are you wearing your ballistic vest?" His eyes remained on my face rather than traveling to my chest for a visual verification.

"Of course." I might be a rookie but I wasn't an idiot. I was miffed, however, that he hadn't seized the opportunity to check out my small but perky rack. Evidently, he took the sexual harassment training more seriously than I did.

He stood and slid into his black suit jacket. He could pull off the upscale executive look as well as he managed the bad-boy façade. Which persona was more like the real Javier Carrasco? There was no way of telling. His armor was soldered solid. No chinks to give anything away.

We made our way down the corridor to the glass doors that led to the elevator lobby. To my surprise, Rasco reached around me to grab the door handle and held it open as I went through. Rasco's gentlemanly gesture made the woman in me sigh in feminine appreciation. One of the downsides to being tall was that men tended to treat me like one of the guys.

I jabbed the down button and turned to Rasco to share the plan I'd made for this mission. "So, I was thinking—"

"You and I will pretend to be a couple shopping for a Christmas present for my mother," he said. "I've asked for your help choosing a gift."

Hot anger colored my cheeks. *What the hell?* Did he not expect me to have thought this through and made plans for our cover? This was *my* meeting, after all. I was the one who'd received the e-mail, not him. Rasco was only along to provide an extra measure of protection. *Babysitting*, wasn't that how he'd put it?

"Call me Robert," he continued. "I'll call you—"

"Princess Guinevere." I raised a cupped hand into the air

and rotated it, princess-in-a-royal-carriage style. Even the office sweetheart was entitled to an occasional snarky comment.

"I'll settle for *Gwen*," he compromised with a glower. "Before we go into the building, we need to do a full outside assessment. Once we're inside, we should both keep a lookout for anything suspicious."

My thought of *Duh!* echoed so loud in my head it was a miracle he didn't hear it.

"The code word if we need to abort the meet-up will be—"

"Sugarplums!" I supplied. With the holidays looming on the horizon, the word seemed fitting.

Rasco exhaled a long breath. Before he could say anything more, the elevator arrived. We stepped on, joining another agent carrying a briefcase and talking to someone via his Bluetooth earpiece.

After we'd descended and exited into the building's main lobby, Rasco turned to me. "Are you always so unprofessional?"

Unprofessional? How dare he! I was tempted to put my knee in *his* sugarplums. "I am *never* unprofessional," I spat back. "Our jobs are intense. We need to have fun once in a while, let off some steam."

Many agents burned out. The dangers, long hours, and stress of being forced to make snap life-or-death decisions without complete information took their toll. My attempts at levity were simply a way of coping, not a sign of incompetence on my part. If Javier would take the time to get to know me better, he'd realize that.

Although he said nothing, Rasco seemed to accept my explanation even if he didn't agree with my methods. "Let's get moving."

"I'll drive." I yanked my keys from my purse and held them up before he could protest.

We stepped outside into a brisk winter day. My nipples peaked inside my lace bra, nature's temperature sensors. Good thing I wore a thick navy blazer so Rasco wouldn't notice.

We climbed into the four-door Mercury Grand Marquis Beldaccio had assigned to me. This particular car had been used by virtually every agent in the office at one point or another and was the blight of the fleet. The car had 263,000 miles on it and nearly as many scratches and dings. It retained only a single hubcap. At speeds over 30 miles per hour, it shook as if suffering a vehicular form of Parkinson's disease. I supposed the color could be called "champagne," but it was more like ginger ale that had gone flat. I found it difficult to feel like a hard-hitting federal agent in a car better suited for a grandmother driving her grandkids to a piano lesson. At least "Granny" had a decent stereo.

I turned south onto Stemmons Freeway, sliding my Pink CD into the player, singing along and pumping an occasional fist as she belted out her hit "So What." Nothing like a good feminist anthem to get a girl in the mood for a possible physical clash.

Rasco glanced my way. "Why do I feel like I'm at a pep rally?"

"This song rocks!" I said. "You can't deny you feel more motivated."

He grunted derisively. Translation: *I was right.* Hee-hee!

Sufficiently revved up now, I turned into a parking lot downtown, slipping the attendant the ten-dollar fee through the window and selecting a spot near the back.

As we walked from the parking lot to the store, I peppered Javier with questions. "What's your mother like?"

"Why do you need to know that?"

"If I'm going to help you choose a Christmas gift for your mother, I need to know something about her."

"You're taking this undercover thing a little too far, aren't

12 DIANE KELLY

you?"

"Now who's being unprofessional?" I snapped. "If we're going to play roles here, let's do it right."

He stopped walking and stared at me for a moment, as if shocked I'd had the guts to stand up to him. Given his physical stature and *don't-mess-with-me* demeanor, I supposed not many people did. But a she-monster like me didn't scare easily. I stopped, too, and stared right back at him. With Javier and I being the same height, our gazes met eye-to-eye. Call me crazy, but after the initial flare of anger cooled off, I saw something else in his eyes. Respect, maybe? Perhaps even a hint of amusement?

When we'd held the gaze too long for my comfort, I turned and continued down the sidewalk. Rasco stepped up and fell in beside me, his strides matching mine.

"About your mother," I said. "What kind of woman is she? Frilly? Practical? Trendy? Old-fashioned?"

He didn't respond right away and, when he did, he surprised me by telling what could have only been the truth. "My mother raised me and my sister on her own after my father was stabbed to death by an addict who robbed him for drug money. The life insurance didn't go far and my mother had to work two jobs to make ends meet. In the daytime she worked as a nurse assistant at a hospital and at night she worked as a caregiver to an elderly couple in our neighborhood. She went without so my sister and I could have what we needed." His hesitated a moment, and when he spoke again his voice was softer. "I once saw her use duct tape to patch a hole in the sole of her work shoe."

Whoa.

What he'd said explained so much. His no-nonsense demeanor. His loner mentality. His single-minded drive to put drug pushers behind bars.

I looked over at him but he turned his head away, as if

he'd revealed more than he'd intended and felt exposed. Maybe even embarrassed.

I spread my fingers to form jazz hands and performed an improvised tap dance on the sidewalk. "Shoes it is."

"What?!" Javier stepped in front of me and faced me down with a look of angry incredulity. "How can you joke—" He stopped himself and his expression transformed into one of understanding. He must've noticed the empathy and compassion in my eyes and realized I hadn't been trying to make light of his tragic childhood, I'd simply been trying to make the discussion less painful and uncomfortable, for both of us. As he gazed at me, his eyes once again became liquid chocolate. My insides melted, too, pooling in my feet.

He turned around and we continued on in our matching rhythm. When we reached the corner across the street from Neiman's, we slowed down. Carefully, we circumnavigated the store, our eyes discreetly searching for signs of a trap.

"See anything?" I whispered.

"What about that homeless guy?" Rasco asked.

A few yards up the sidewalk a bearded homeless man wearing a filthy knit cap pushed a shopping cart our way. Rasco slid his hand inside his jacket, ready to pull his gun if need be. I slipped my hand into my purse, found my weapon, and steeled myself.

As the man neared us without changing pace or reaching for anything inside the basket, I realized our suspicions had been unfounded. Besides, his stench was too well developed for him to be a decoy. My hand moved from my gun and instead pulled a candy cane from my purse. I handed it to the man. "Happy holidays!"

He responded with a gap-toothed smile. "You, too, sweetie!"

Javier shook his head.

Satisfied the doors weren't under observation from the outside, Javier and I crossed the street and entered the store.

The place was decked out in holiday splendor, with flocked Christmas trees spaced here and there and glittery snowflakes hanging from the ceiling. Twinkle lights encircled the columns and holiday music streamed through the store's stereo speakers, completing the festive atmosphere.

Javier and I rode the escalator to the second floor, which housed the shoe department and women's apparel. We weaved our way past the fragrant cosmetics counters to the shoe section.

"What size does your mother wear?" I asked as we meandered along the perimeter, checking out the offerings.

Rasco shrugged. "Not sure. I recall her once remarking that she wore the same size as that Kardashian woman who's on all the magazines."

I whipped out my phone and performed a Google search. Depending on which Kardashian his mother had been referring to, the size could be a 5, 7, or 10. "Which Kardashian?" I asked. "Kim? Kourtney? Khloé?"

His brows drew together. "There's more than one of them?"

I didn't hold back the eye roll this time. You'd think a federal investigator would have better observation skills. I shoved my phone back into my purse. "Let's go about this another way. How does her foot compare to mine?"

I held up one of my feet, clad in a stylish loafer, size 11.

Rasco's brows lifted. "Is that a foot or a ski?"

I simulated a roundhouse kick. "It's a lethal weapon."

Before I could pull my foot back he caught me by the ankle, forcing me to hop on one leg to maintain my balance. His lips curved up in an undeniable grin now, revealing his perfect teeth. *God, he should smile more often. I mean, that mouth . . .*

When he released me, the skin around my ankle was warm from his touch. I tried not to feel disappointed as the sensation faded.

FIVE GOLD-SMUGGLING RINGS   **15**

"My mother's feet are much smaller than yours," Rasco said, back to the business at hand. Or should I say the business at *foot*? "Maybe half your size."

Again with the urge to plant my knee in his sugarplums.

"Text your sister," I suggested. "She'll know the exact size."

He pulled out his phone, typed a text, and in seconds we had a definitive answer.

Seven.

Armed with this information, we launched our search for the perfect shoe. Rasco began nosing around in the sensible shoes, the lower-heeled, less glamorous styles worn by former fashionistas now dealing with arthritis and bunions.

I grabbed a gray flat from his hand and returned it to the display. "No way, José. That shoe screams 'boring!' Your mother deserves something fun and sexy."

His nose crinkled. "I don't want to think of my mother as sexy."

"*You* might not, but trust me. *She* does."

After ten minutes of cajoling on my part, I convinced him to purchase a pair of four-inch sparkling red stilettos. "Send them to your mom right away and tell her to open them early. She might have a special holiday party to wear them to."

"The only holiday event she attends is midnight Mass."

"Well, then," I said, "she'll be the hottest woman in line for Communion."

Rasco frowned. "That seems . . . *wrong*."

"God will get over it."

"Or send her straight to hell."

"She'll have company," I said. "I'm getting a pair, too."

CHAPTER 3

DOES THIS INVESTIGATION MAKE MY BUTT LOOK BIG?

A seasoned saleslady stepped over. "Can I help you two?"

Javier held up the shoe. "I need a pair of these in a size seven."

"And I need an eleven if you've got them." I could hardly afford to spend $120 on shoes, but they lured me in like a stiletto siren call onto the banks of bankruptcy.

"Great!" The clerk smiled as the *cha-ching* of a sizeable commission rang up in her head. "I'll be right back."

I hoped they'd have my size. The shoes would be perfect for New Year's Eve. While I had no date as yet, a girl can always hope, can't she? Besides, my girlfriends had a pact. Anyone without a date on New Year's would get dolled up anyway and meet the others at the Rattlesnake Bar in the Ritz-Carlton hotel. The drink prices were outrageous—just like they were in any bar worth going to in the Big D—but the view of the downtown skyline was breathtaking and the sophisticated clientele more likely to give you stock tips than an STD. The same could not be said of the meat-market type nightclubs.

FIVE GOLD-SMUGGLING RINGS **17**

The clerk returned with the shoes. "Got 'em!"

I slipped out of my loafers and socks and into the stilettos. A woman who stood over six feet barefoot probably had no business adding another four inches to her stature, but convention never stopped me before.

"Wow," the saleslady said. "Those shoes look divine on you."

I'd learned the hard way never to trust a salesperson who worked on a percentage.

I stepped over to the mirror to see for myself. The saleslady hadn't lied. The shoes did indeed look divine. What's more, the steep angle made my enormous feet appear much smaller than actual size. *Damn girl*, I told my reflection. *You look fine!*

In the mirror I spotted Javier behind me, his gaze working its way up from the shoes and lingering on my butt. *So, he's an ass man, huh?* When our gazes met in the mirror he quickly looked away. And to think *he* had accused *me* of being unprofessional. Not that I'd minded the ogling one bit. Then again, I shouldn't read anything into the way he'd looked at me. He was a man, after all, and when there's a female ass in the vicinity they are programmed by their caveman DNA to check it out. I shouldn't take it personally.

But I *wanted* to take it personally.

"What do you think?" I asked. After all, we were pretending to be a couple and if he were actually my boyfriend I would have asked his opinion. I would have also promptly ignored his opinion if it conflicted with my own.

He swallowed hard as if forcing down thoughts he feared might spill out of his mouth. "You look . . . nice."

"Nice?" I snorted. "I don't look *nice*. I look hotter than hell."

Javier damn well knew it, too. What's more, I think he knew I knew he knew it.

18   DIANE KELLY

I whipped out my wallet and handed my Visa card to the clerk. "I'll take them."

Our shoe shopping now complete, Rasco and I continued to the evening-gown department. When another saleslady approached, I told her I was "just browsing." Fortunately, she took the hint and left us alone.

As we wandered about, we kept an eye out for anyone watching us. Although a few sent the usual *holy-shit-she's-tall!* looks my way, nobody seemed especially interested.

My eye settled on a standard black cocktail dress in my size. As long as we were pretending to be a couple, might as well play it up, right? I pulled the dress from the rack and held it in front of me. "What do you think?"

Rasco's eyes roamed over my body, making me feel naked and vulnerable despite being fully dressed and holding an additional layer of clothing over me. My memory banks horked up another memory of me in a fancy dress, a painful memory that had left me with the same vulnerable feeling. *The homecoming dance, freshman year of high school.* One of the basketball players had asked me to go with him and I'd been thrilled. Unfortunately, the thrill was short lived. All it took was his dumb-ass teammate asking if I'd been assembled by a mad scientist in a laboratory and the fun was over. For me, anyway. My date and his friends had laughed hysterically. I'd forced a laugh along with them, but soon afterward feigned a headache and walked home by myself, staying in the shadows so nobody could see me cry.

Assholes.

Rasco reached out for the dress in my hands, checked the tag for the size, and turned to pull a dress from another rack. "Try this red one. It'll go better with the shoes. Besides, it's—"

He stopped himself.

"It's *what*?" I prodded.

His forehead furrowed as he seemed to search for the right words. "It's . . . different from the others."

As I took the dress from him, our eyes met again and held for a moment. His comment about the red dress, that it was different, there had been a subtle subtext there, right? He'd implied that I, too, was different. The only question now was whether his words and actions had been sincere, or merely part of our undercover act. If they were just part of the act, he'd played his part like a pro. Someone should give the guy a Tony Award. But maybe, just maybe, I was beginning to grow on the guy …

"I'll go try these on."

I headed toward the dressing rooms, Rasco trailing behind. As we approached, we noticed two dark-skinned men waiting near the entrance. They were dressed in dapper three-piece suits, complete with colorful silk ties and matching pocket squares. Their height and well-developed musculature made it clear these were no everyday shoppers.

"Bodyguards," Rasco whispered. "Meet me in cosmetics when you're done."

Fortunately, the two hadn't spotted us. One looked down at his cell phone screen, probably checking e-mails or surfing the Internet. The other scanned the area, but hadn't yet turned our way.

Rasco vectored off toward cosmetics, while I sneaked into the dressing rooms. My steps slowed once I'd cleared the entrance. Noting a pair of tiny feet under one of the doors, I rustled the dresses to make my presence known.

A moment later, the slatted door opened a couple of inches and the face of a young woman peeked through. She had the high, enviable cheekbones typical of Congolese women.

"Bon jour, Agent Dietrich," she whispered in a voice tinged with a French accent. She quietly opened the door and gestured for me to come into the room with her. Once I had, she shut the door behind me.

The woman appeared to be around twenty years old. Her features were delicate, her long black hair hanging in thin braids down her back. She stood five feet tall and weighed approximately the same as a butterfly. In the small space, one wrong move and I'd accidentally squash her.

She was dressed in an emerald-green floor-length gown trimmed with iridescent sequins. It was a beautiful dress, but I'd look like the Jolly Green Giant in it. A dozen more evening gowns dangled from hooks inside the room. The tags noted they were size two. *Seriously?* I hung my circus tent-sized dresses next to them. The woman gestured for me to take a seat on the bench. Perhaps she, too, feared I'd squash her.

With me sitting and her standing, we were the same height.

She held out her hand. "I'm Nicia Kayembe," she whispered.

I took her tiny hand in my large one, careful not to crush her fingers. "Why did you ask me to meet you, Nicia?"

"I saw your video online," she said, wasting no time. "You took down a smuggler with a fire extinguisher."

That fire extinguisher would forever be my claim to fame.

"With my bodyguards always nearby," Nicia continued, "I knew I would only be able to speak privately with a female agent. I also believed a woman would be more inclined to help."

"Help with what, exactly?"

She took a step closer and lowered her voice further. "My father is Aristide Kayembe, the deputy economic minister for the Democratic Republic of the Congo. He has brought gold into this country in his plane. Five small black suitcases filled with it. He did not disclose the gold to the American government. This is illegal, no?"

"You're correct. American law requires the gold be disclosed."

Because gold could be moved without leaving a paper trail, federal law required that gold bullion and coins be declared to ICE upon entry. If the gold was in the form of currency valued at $10,000 or more, the party was also required to file a financial disclosure form with the Treasury Department. These measures were designed to track the movement of gold and prevent its use in money laundering and financing terrorism.

As I'd learned in training, gold smuggling was on the rise. To curb its trade deficit, India had repeatedly increased its import duty on gold. Last I heard the going rate was a steep 10%. Crafty dealers looking to avoid the tariffs had begun smuggling gold into the country, many taking routes through Pakistan, which imposed no duty on gold imports. Pakistan, in turn, had imposed a temporary moratorium on gold imports in an effort to stop smugglers from using the country as a way station.

"How do you know about the suitcases?" I asked. "About the gold?"

"Just after I boarded the plane, I realized I had left my earphones in my luggage. I saw the staff loading the suitcases into the cargo bay when I went to retrieve my earphones. I was curious what was inside, so I peeked into one of them when the men had their backs turned."

I mentally weighed the information. The Congo was known for its smuggling rings. Diamonds. Coffee. Ivory. Gold. Poverty led some to engage in illegal activities, though much of the smuggling was done by wealthier members of Congolese society. It was possible Nicia's father was using his political connections to smuggle gold out of his country and into the United States. Despite the apparent veracity of her story, I knew informants were not always reliable. Their motives could be malicious. Some lied outright to send agents scurrying down bunny trails or to make the U.S. government look bad when it launched a raid that turned up nothing.

I watched her closely to gauge her reaction. "Why are you telling me this?"

"Because my father is a bastard," she spat in that way only

an indignant daughter can. "He is using his position for his own gain."

She explained that her father was in cahoots with warlords who oversaw gold mines in certain parts of the country. The miners worked in deplorable conditions and were paid a pittance for their hard labor. If they were caught pocketing even a tiny nugget of the gold they worked so hard to mine, they'd lose a hand . . . *or worse.*

"The warlords use gold to pay for weapons and soldiers to continue their senseless fighting. Meanwhile, women in my country are being raped and people are starving."

Though "conflict gold" had yet to receive the press given to blood diamonds, the results were the same. The poor were oppressed through threats of violence and the country's resources, which could provide good incomes to many, were instead exploited by a privileged, powerful few.

"Have you told your father how you feel?"

"Many times." Nicia's hands fisted in frustration. "But he will not listen to me. He does not care how I feel."

Nicia said that she and her peers wanted a better future for themselves and their country. Her eyes gleamed as if she could visualize the bright future she dreamed of. "But we will never have it if this type of corruption continues." She took my hands in hers and turned pleading eyes on me. "You can seize the gold? Impound the plane? Have my father arrested?"

I hated to disappoint her, but I had to be honest. "I'm sorry, Nicia. Even if he's done something illegal, I can't search his plane or arrest him. He's protected by diplomatic immunity."

She released a sharp breath. Her expression became desperate and her grip on my hands tightened. "But you will do something, no? Please! You must!"

This was not only a chance to have a case of my own, but

also to put a stop to fraud and exploitation. Perhaps, in some small way, the case could further the interests of the Congolese people.

"I'll look into it," I said, "but I can't make any promises."

"I understand." Nicia gave me an encouraging smile. "We can only try our best. I will continue to do what I can from the inside. Thank you, Agent Dietrich." With a squeeze to seal our pact, she released my hands.

"Do you know when the gold will change hands?"

"I overheard my father speaking to Jean Paul, the pilot, and Rodrigue, the copilot. He instructed them to stay with the plane all day Thursday and on Friday morning so that his business associates could pick up their 'gifts.'" She formed air quotes with her fingers. "That is why I contacted you, because the people who will receive the gold are here in Dallas."

"Any idea who these business associates are?"

"No. When we make these trips to America my father sends me out to shop and sightsee. He never includes me in his business affairs."

"How often does your father come to Dallas?"

"About four times a year."

"Where does he stay here?"

"Most often in the Renaissance hotel," she said, "though we have stayed other places downtown a time or two."

"Where is his plane now?"

"In a rented hangar at the Dallas-Fort Worth Airport."

"Has your father planned your return to Kinshasa?"

Nicia nodded. "We fly out Friday at noon." Fearing reprisal, Nicia wanted no one to know she had spilled the beans about the gold. "If my father found out I talked to you, I do not know what would become of me."

I couldn't bear the thought of being responsible if she were locked away or hurt. I'd find another way to build a case against the smugglers.

24   DIANE KELLY

"One more question," Nicia added. She turned away from me, looking back over her shoulder. "Does this dress make my butt look big?"

CHAPTER 4

NOT JUST ALONG FOR THE RIDE

After assuring Nicia she'd have to gain fifty pounds before her butt would be even average sized, I slipped into another dressing room and tried on the red dress. It was a flirty style, with a sweetheart neckline, vertical ruffles on the knee-length skirt, and spaghetti straps that crossed in back. Rasco was right. It wasn't typical at all. It fit perfectly, as if made for me. I slid my feet into the stilettos and stepped out of my dressing room.

Nicia stood in front of the three-way mirror at the end of the row, turning this way and that as she looked over the midnight-blue gown she wore now. When she noticed me, she put her hands over her mouth. "Oh, my goodness!" she cried. "You are beautiful!"

"I know, right?" The pantsuit I'd been wearing earlier hadn't done much for me, but this dress was an entirely different story. Despite my size, I looked feminine and elegant, more like a supermodel than a she-monster.

I returned to my fitting room and took one final look at my glorious self in the mirror. After slipping back out of the dress, I checked the price tag. $379. It took me only a moment to decide I was worth it. If I ate ramen noodles for dinner every night for a month and turned the heat in my apartment down to 50 degrees, I could make up for this splurge.

I waited for several minutes after Nicia had exited the fitting rooms, allowing her time to complete her purchases and leave the store with her bodyguards. After I paid for my dress, Rasco and I returned to my car. On the way, I gave him the scoop regarding my conversation with Nicia.

"This could be big," he said. "I want in."

He wouldn't have to ask me twice. "Deal."

Once we were in the car, I aimed straight for the downtown post office and pulled into the lot.

"Go mail the shoes to your mom," I demanded. After losing her husband and raising two kids on her own, his mother deserved the frivolous footwear. Rasco still didn't seem entirely convinced. I wasn't about to give him a chance to change his mind. I pointed to the front door of the building. "Now."

"You're bossy," Rasco snapped.

"Only when I'm right."

Shooting me a final narrowed-eye glance, he went inside, returning ten minutes later empty handed. "I can't believe I let you talk me into buying those shoes."

I wondered what else I might be able to talk him into . . . *or out of*. His pants, for instance.

We'd driven halfway back to the office when his cell phone rang, blaring the Vanilla Ice classic "Ice Ice Baby." Funny, I had the same ringtone. Of course, so did half the agents in the office, but still.

He thumbed the screen to accept the call and put the phone to his ear. "Agent Carrasco." After a short pause, his free hand went to his head and clenched his skull in a death grip. "This can't be happening! Guerra wasn't supposed to move the stash until tonight." Another pause. "I'm on my way." He ended the call and turned to me. "Head to Oak Cliff. Now!"

FIVE GOLD-SMUGGLING RINGS   27

I swerved across three lanes of traffic, barely making the exit and earning two honks and a raised middle finger. We circled around the overpass. Javier navigated as we sped south down the freeway.

"I've been working with a joint task force of local cops and DEA agents to bust up the cartel," he explained. "We knew they had a major distribution center here in Dallas. We narrowed the storage site to a house in Oak Cliff and got a wiretap on their phones. Earlier communications indicated they planned to move the drugs to a new location tonight."

He went on to say that a neighbor had complained about cars coming and going late at night and threatened to call police. The dealers feared the neighbor would make good on the threats and their operation would be discovered.

Rasco wriggled out of his suit jacket and draped it over the seat between us. His tie came off next.

I glanced over at him. "If you're expecting me to tuck a dollar into your belt you've got another thing coming."

He shot a look my way. "I can't take down dealers in this monkey suit. It's too confining."

"Got your raid jacket with you?"

"No," he replied. "It's back at the office."

Given that some undercover agents looked no different than dealers, it was easy to get the two confused in the heat of a bust. More than one agent had been injured by friendly fire. To prevent misidentification, and to ensure the bad guys could be prosecuted for assault on federal agents, operatives were required to wear jackets with the words ICE–POLICE in large print on the back and front.

"Here." I reached over the seat to grab my jacket from the back. I tossed it into his lap. "Use mine."

"Thanks." He slipped it on, then stared through the windshield as if fixated on something in the distance. The guy was always intense, but the look in his eyes was more than simple concentration. It was haunted, maybe even obsessed.

"You all right?"

Still staring straight ahead, Javier said, "Enrique Guerra's the head of the cartel here. He used to be a dealer in Tucson but relocated here when he was promoted within the cartel. He's the reason I transferred to Dallas."

I had a sneaking hunch about Guerra. "He sold drugs to the addict who killed your father."

After a shuddering breath, Javier dipped his chin in acknowledgment. "I vowed I'd get Guerra. No matter how long it took. This is the closest I've ever come." His voice took on a desperate edge. "I can't let him get away!"

"He won't." I reached out and gave his hand an encouraging squeeze just as Nicia had done to me earlier. "You'll get him."

To my surprise, Javier put his other hand over mine. It was an act of solidarity. But dare I dream it could also be a sign of burgeoning attraction?

With my size 11's putting the pedal to the metal, we arrived on the scene in mere minutes. Rasco met up with his team a block from the house. While I huddled inside the warm car, they huddled outside in the cold, reviewing their game plan. Though I wasn't officially a part of this bust I unrolled my window to listen. Like Beldaccio said, this could be a learning experience for me. Unfortunately, the agents spoke too softly for me to hear much, but it was clear from the looks on their faces they were ready to kick ass.

When they finished speaking, Rasco stepped up to my window, his jaw clenched. "Guerra isn't here."

Damn. "You'll get him next time."

"If he gets wind of this operation he'll disappear. There won't be a next time." The bulging vein in his neck said he was ready to explode in frustration. "But we've got to go in now or we risk losing the other dealers and the evidence."

I raised my hand to offer him a good-luck fist bump. "Go get 'em, cowboy."

FIVE GOLD-SMUGGLING RINGS   29

He bumped my fist with his own and turned to go.

As I watched from my car, a dozen armed agents surrounded a dilapidated wood-frame house. In an apparent attempt to make the house look like a normal residence, someone had hung a Christmas wreath on the front door. I wondered whether it was made of holly, pine, or marijuana. *Deck the halls with boughs of reefer . . .*

A team of four men followed Rasco through the front yard. They crouched low, trying to stay out of view should someone inside glance out a window. Knowing Javier was leading what could be a suicide mission, I held my breath.

Rasco stuck his hand out to his side, three fingers extended. He retracted each finger as he silently counted down. I silently counted down with him.

Three.

Two.

One.

His gun clutched in front of him, Rasco stormed the porch, banged three times on the door with his fist, and hollered, "Federal agents!" He turned sideways next to the jamb in case those inside attempted to shoot through the door.

No response came. The minions in the house were either hiding the evidence, preparing to make an escape attempt, or rounding up their weapons for an all-out war. I hoped it wasn't the latter.

Two DEA agents in full protective gear ran up the steps. It took them three tries to kick in the reinforced door. With my big feet I could've done it in one.

The Christmas wreath fell to the ground. Rasco kicked it aside. The entry open, the men disappeared inside.

My stomach retracted into a hard stone. Would I ever see Javier alive again?

CHAPTER 5
POLAR BEAR PLUNGE

My heart seemed to stop beating as I listened. A blissful silence hung in the air for a moment. *Thank goodness.* It seemed as if Guerra's minions would go down without a fight.

Pop-pop-pop!

Gunfire! *Damn. I'd spoken too soon.* But who had fired the gun? And who had been hit?

As I sat there with every muscle in my body tensed, a shiny black Mercedes SUV pulled to the curb opposite me. It was a GL550 model, with a V-8 biturbo engine. Lots of power under that hood. Along with the big engine came a big price tag. Nearly ninety grand brand new. The car cost more than most houses in this neighborhood.

At the wheel sat a Latino man sporting sunglasses. Odd, since the day was overcast. He looked down the street at the drug house. I followed his gaze. The door hung open and agents were visible hunkered down behind trash cans and cars, ready to pick off any dealers who attempted an escape.

The man in the SUV threw the gearshift into reverse and backed into a driveway. When he attempted to drive forward, he found a federal agent standing in front of him, a gun aimed at him through the windshield. That agent was me. It didn't take a Harvard graduate to figure out this guy was the boss of the drug operation. If Guerra thought he was getting away, he better think again.

"Federal agent!" I yelled. "Out of the car! Now!"

The dumb ass didn't listen, though, as dumb asses are wont to do.

With a screech of tires, he floored the gas pedal and came at me. I could have shot him through the windshield, but even if I managed to kill Guerra the car would plow me down. I didn't want to end up as roadkill. I really should have thought this through first.

Pulling up long-latent muscle memory from my pole-vaulting days, I leaped upward and backward as the car came at me, landing on my back on the hood. The metal gave in under my weight. *Kuhklunk!*

Momentum slammed me into the windshield, my ribs nearly cracking on impact. With my free hand, I reached up and grabbed the front bar of the luggage rack to steady myself. As Guerra careened down the street with me surfing on his hood, I swung myself up onto the roof of the SUV, falling face-first toward the tailgate.

He floored the gas, roaring down the street while I sprawled across the luggage rack, clutching the back bar with my hands and leveraging my feet in the front corners. Two blocks behind us, Javier stepped into the street, waving his arms to let me know he'd spotted me on the SUV's roof. Looked like he'd survived this bust. I hoped I'd do the same.

Guerra jerked the wheel side to side, attempting to throw me from the roof. Luckily, the streets were narrow and cars were parked along each side, giving Guerra limited space to maneuver. I held on for dear life.

Strange things go through your mind when you are facing death. My first thought was *What outfit will my mother bury me in?* Dear God, don't let it be that hideous peach-colored shift she'd forced on me last time we'd gone shopping together. *Will my cat be happy living with my sister?* I hoped she'd remember that Mister Mow-Mow preferred canned tuna to dry kibble. *What kind of rollover rating does this car have?* I prayed it was five stars. It was bad enough I had a hopeless crush on Rasco. Being actually crushed would totally suck.

Given my assumptions that Guerra was armed and would try to avoid rolling the vehicle lest he injure himself, my biggest fear was that he'd shoot me through the roof. *Ack!* I hoped he didn't think of that. Kinda wished I hadn't either . . .

Blam!

Damn! He'd thought of it, too. I looked back to see a hole in the roof between my ankles. Thank God he'd missed me.

Blam!

Another hole appeared, this one between my calves. He was moving up my legs. Uh-oh.

Blam!

This time the hole appeared between my knees. I figured there would be one more shot between my thighs before he put a hole through my girly business.

Blam!

There it was. The thigh shot. One more bullet and there'd be serious damage to my fun parts. *Seriously, why hasn't someone invented ballistic panties?*

I had a tough choice to make. On one hand, I could return fire. Doing so would require me to take my right hand off the luggage rack and posed the risk I'd be thrown from the roof of the SUV. One other hand, I could try to get into position to safely jump from the car. Unfortunately, I was not a Teenage Mutant Ninja Turtle and was more likely to splatter to the pavement in the path of an oncoming bus than to roll safely across a yard. On the third hand, I could steel myself for the inevitable and hope a prosthetics engineer or sex toy company would invent a strap-on vagina to replace my bullet-ridden nether regions.

Hmm . . .

Return fire it was.

I aimed my gun to the left of the first bullet hole and squeezed off three rounds.

Bang-bang-bang!

My shots were followed by the *tinkle* of glass as the windshield shattered. The SUV lurched forward before turning to the right, hopping a curb, and mowing down a life-size plastic Nativity yard display. Joseph was flattened, the Virgin Mary was knocked aside, and the baby Jesus was sent airborne, as if ascending prematurely to the heavens. The car continued on, rolling into a backyard and colliding with an above-ground pool filled with leaves and murky water.

Sploosh!

The impact sent a geyser of water over the opposite edge of the pool. Unfortunately, a moment later, the laws of physics sent a surge of water rocketing back my way. A tsunami of ice-cold chlorinated water spilled over the SUV, dousing me from toe to head. "Shit!"

When I caught my breath, I pushed myself up on the roof of the car and knelt there, trying to gather my wits.

The door of the SUV swung open and the driver emerged, shards of glass in his face and three bloody holes in his right shoulder. He glanced around, as if trying to determine the best avenue of escape. A waste of time, really. This guy wasn't going anywhere. Not if I had anything to say about it.

He'd taken just two steps when I leaped from the roof of the SUV onto his back. Okay, so maybe yelling "Geronimo!" was childish, but if you can't enjoy your work, why do it?

Poomph. The two of us hit the ground, the man taking the brunt of the impact. How courteous of him. *Who says chivalry is dead?*

We wrestled on the ground, blood seeping from his

injuries and staining the sleeve of my blazer. *Ew.* I hoped he'd had all of his shots. Didn't want to catch a case of the *bah-humbugs.*

The man managed to escape my clutches and push himself to a wobbly stand. Luckily for me, he appeared to be unarmed. Probably the airbag had knocked the gun from his hand. Unluckily for me, my gun had flown out of my hand, too, when we'd hit the pool. The two of us would have to go at this *mano a mano.* Or should I say *mano a womano?*

He threw a left hook at my jaw. I jerked my head back just in time for his swing to pass an inch in front of my face. I could have returned the punch but why risk sore knuckles? A swift lift of my size 11's and Guerra's chestnuts were cracked and ready for roasting over an open fire. He collapsed to the ground, his hands over his tenderized crotch.

I bent down and attempted to search his pockets for additional weapons but, with the man whipping from side to side and kicking out at me, a pat-down proved impossible. My handcuffs were in my purse back in my granny-mobile. I glanced around, hoping to locate my Glock, Guerra's gun, or something I could use to shackle the man. The only thing my eyes spied were several strings of colored Christmas lights wrapped around a nearby tree.

As quickly as I could, I unwrapped a strand of lights from a branch, keeping one eye on the writhing Guerra all the while. When I bent to unplug the string of lights from the adjoining strand, I averted my gaze from Guerra for one brief moment. Unfortunately, one brief moment was all it took for him to pull a second weapon he must have had hidden in his pocket. I turned to find him standing with his gun aimed at my face at point-blank range.

Before I could react, a dark blur streaked past me and tackled Guerra to the ground.

Javier.

And not a second too soon.

The two men wrangled in an all-out brawl. In seconds, Rasco had wrestled Guerra's gun out of his hand, pinned the man under him, and begun delivering a series of punches to Guerra's face. Guerra deserved every one of them and more. Before he got all he had coming to him, the kingpin begged for mercy.

"Stop!" Guerra screamed. "I give up!"

Rasco stood and stared down at the man responsible for his father's death. A mix of emotions played across his face. Sorrow. Loss. Relief. Rage. He aimed Guerra's gun at the man's face. "My father was killed by an addict who robbed *him* to buy drugs from *you*." Though his voice was deceptively calm, Javier's hand shook as he restrained himself from shooting the man at his feet. "Give me one good reason why I shouldn't blow your brains out."

The world seemed to stop turning.

I stepped over to Javier's side. "He deserves to die," I said softly. "But ICE needs you to put more guys like him out of business."

What's more, if Rasco shot this bastard, he'd end up in jail himself. After everything he'd lost already, he didn't need to lose his job and freedom, too.

I reached over to push Javier's arm down. He resisted and we engaged in a brief battle of muscle and will before he finally acquiesced. Without looking my way, he handed the gun to me and pulled his handcuffs from his pocket to shackle Guerra.

The crisis resolved and the suspect in restraints, I bent over, my hands on my knees.

Javier turned to me. "You okay?"

"I'm fine." Couple of broken ribs, maybe, but nothing a physician couldn't patch up on an outpatient basis. Maybe the doc would even give me some high-powered painkillers. Nothing like some oxycodone to put a person in the holiday spirit. *Joy to the world!*

Javier used his foot to push Guerra over onto his stomach and ordered him to remain face down in the dirt. Stepping to the door of the SUV, he peered inside and muttered, "Jesus."

"Find a stash?" I asked. "More weapons?"

"No." He pulled the plastic baby Jesus out of the cab and held it up. "I was referring to this."

While the drug dealer might be pocked with glass and full of bullets, the made-in-China plastic Messiah didn't have a scratch on him, despite having been hit by the car and tossed into the air, only to fall through a shattered windshield. It was either a Christmas miracle or a testament to Chinese manufacturing.

While the other agents hauled Guerra and his dealers away, Rasco drove me to the ER in the Marquis. Even with the heater running full blast and my raid jacket draped over me, my teeth chattered thanks to my soaking-wet clothes. The only thing I had in my car to change into was my new cocktail dress, but I'd rather suffer hypothermia than risk damaging the gorgeous thing by putting it on my chlorine-doused body. Rasco offered his suit jacket, but I declined for the same reason. No sense ruining his sport coat. "Just drive fast."

An hour later, as I sat on the crinkly paper of the exam table, the doctor delivered his diagnoses—bruised ribs and temporary insanity.

He frowned. "What possessed you to jump on top of a moving car?"

I shrugged, cringing when the motion sent a twinge of pain across my side. "It seemed like the thing to do at the time."

He prescribed no pain meds, only bed rest and aspirin. *Party pooper.*

I left the hospital wearing a thin hospital gown and a pair of cheap paper booties. Lest I accidentally moon someone on my way out, the nurse had also given me a blanket to wrap

FIVE GOLD-SMUGGLING RINGS   37

around myself. My suit and shoes were in the trash, unsalvageable.

By the time Javier and I made it back to the office, it was 7:00 pm. Rasco helped me out of Granny and into my pickup, a purchase I'd made not so much for its cargo capabilities as the head room. It took the king-cab pickup to comfortably accommodate my height, especially when I wore my blond locks swept into a towering updo. Maybe I should get my hair done for New Year's Eve to go along with my gorgeous new dress.

After I'd settled in my seat and clicked my belt into place, Rasco hooked a hand over the top of the window and leaned in. "If you need anything, call me. Guerra would've gotten away today if it wasn't for you." Gratitude gleamed in his eyes. "I owe you, Angelika."

It was the first time Rasco had spoken my name, and the way it rolled off his lips like a drop of sweet honey nearly made me swoon. "Just doing my job." I fought the urge to grab his shirt and pull him in for a kiss. "You can pay me back by helping me bust the gold smugglers."

He dipped his head. "Consider it done."

CHAPTER 6

YOU CAN'T JOIN THE MILE-HIGH CLUB IF YOU DON'T GET OFF THE GROUND

Beldaccio insisted I spend Wednesday at home to rest my sore ribs. But one day on my back was all I could spare. At seven Thursday morning, Rasco and I met at the office to prepare for the day's undercover operation. I cocked my head, eyeing him. He looked different today. The hard edges and emotional distance that had defined him had eased. Arresting Guerra seemed to have lifted a huge weight off Javier's shoulders. He was no less sexy, though, damn him. If anything, his new appearance of accessibility only made me want him more.

I pulled my hair into a ponytail and Rasco slid a ball cap on his head. Over our jeans and T-shirts we donned matching gray coveralls he'd picked up at an automotive supply store. Looking like a drab version of Thing 1 and Thing 2, we headed to the DFW Airport in Rasco's government-issued car, a black Dodge Charger. Much sexier than Granny. Lucky duck. Of course, now that I'd helped nab a major drug dealer, maybe I'd have some leverage for an upgrade.

Javier glanced over at me as he drove. "I called my mother last night and told her we'd finally nailed Guerra. She broke down in tears. She said it was the best Christmas present she'd ever received."

I pretended not to notice that his voice cracked as he relayed the information to me. "Well, then," I said. "The stilettos will be the icing on the cake."

He responded with a soft chuckle.

I'd made arrangements with the airport authorities for us to go undercover as members of a maintenance crew working in the hangar adjacent to the one Aristide Kayembe had rented. The guise would put us in close proximity where we could keep an eye on the comings and goings.

The security guard at the entry gate asked us for identification and looked over his visitor log to make sure our presence had been pre-approved. He hadn't been told the reason for our visit. The fewer people who knew our true identities, the lower the chances of Kayembe realizing the U.S. government was on to his scheme.

"Here are your visitor badges." The guard handed each of us an orange badge with a metal clip to fasten it to our clothing. "Wear them at all times."

We clipped the badges to the breast pocket of our coveralls and he waved us in. Once the gate slid closed behind us and we'd set off for hangar 37, we ripped the badges from our coveralls. No sense sending Kayembe or his staff any signal we didn't belong here.

We drove down the row of wide metal buildings, looking for our unit. When we arrived, we found the large front door open as promised. A Beechcraft Hawker 400 XPR was parked inside, the door open, a set of metal rolling stairs positioned in front of it. The plane, one of several owned by an oil mogul, had been grounded temporarily for routine maintenance. Luckily for us, the mogul had agreed to let us use the hangar and plane as props in our undercover operation.

Although the authorities had assured us Kayembe's plane was located inside hangar 38, we were unable to make an immediate visual verification. All of the doors to the unit were closed tight, for now at least. If Nicia was right, the others involved in Kayembe's smuggling operations should be coming by the hangar to pick up their gold.

Rasco pulled into hangar 37, parking at the back behind the plane. We set about opening the regular-sized back and side doors of the hangar, flipping the stops down hold them in place. Fortunately, the cold snap and clouds had moved east, and today was a higher-than-average 68 degrees. The soft breeze that blew through the space was cool but not cold.

The two of us looked around the hangar. A broom and dustpan stood in the back corner. Three folding chairs sat near the front door of the hangar, providing a vantage point from which to watch planes take off and land. A rolling metal toolbox with several drawers stood against the side wall.

"Let's check out the plane," Javier suggested.

We climbed inside the aircraft to look around. The plane wasn't large, but the seats were luxurious and built to fully recline, like first-class seats on overseas commercial flights.

Javier sat down in one of them and laid it back. "Think anyone has joined the mile-high club in here?"

His joke caught me off guard, and I issued a half gasp, half laugh. I gestured to the chair he was lying in. "Probably in that very seat."

"Yikes." He returned the seat to its upright position and stood.

We continued our self-guided tour. A large-screen television was mounted on a wall at the back, complete with a DVD player and gaming system. A small refrigerator held water, sodas, and a bottle of Cristal champagne.

I snagged the champagne, flopped down in another chair, and leaned back, cuddling the bottle to my chest. "This is the life, huh? A girl could get used to this."

"Not a girl like you." Javier eyed me intently. "You'd be bored."

FIVE GOLD-SMUGGLING RINGS   41

I sighed. "True." I wasn't made to be pampered. I was built for action. Kinda cool that Javier seemed not only to understand that, but also to respect me for it. I returned the champagne to the fridge and exited the plane.

"We've got to look busy." Rasco followed me down the staircase and stepped over to the tool box. He opened the top drawer of and nosed around for a moment before pulling out an old copy of *Hustler Magazine* that had been shoved to the back. He opened the magazine to the centerfold and held it up at an angle. "Wow. This woman is exceptionally limber."

Before I could chastise him, a flash of silver passed by the side door.

CHAPTER 7
OUTSOURCING

I grabbed the broom and pretended to sweep the space while eyeing the Ford Taurus that had parked at the hangar next door. Two dark-skinned men emerged from the vehicle, speaking in French.

The one who'd been driving the car stepped up to the keypad at the entrance and punched in a code. As the door opened, my eyes glimpsed their large white plane. A flag was painted on the door. The blue flag had a gold star in the upper-left corner and a red stripe running diagonally from the bottom left to the upper right. The flag of the DRC. I recognized it from the research I'd performed yesterday.

The two men went inside and the door swung shut behind them.

Rasco sauntered behind me, a wrench in his hand. "Pilot and copilot, I'd say."

My thoughts exactly. Jean Paul and Rodrigue.

Rasco strode to his Charger, where he pulled his tablet from his briefcase. Logging into our ICE research program, he ran the car's license plate number while I kept a discreet eye on the hangar. He looked up when he had the data. "The car's owned by Alamo rental."

FIVE GOLD-SMUGGLING RINGS   43

To be expected, I supposed. Given what Nicia had told me, her father did not maintain regular quarters in Dallas.

There was no activity at hangar 38 for the next two hours. Javier and I had been puttering around the hangar, doing our best to look busy, when a blue BMW with tinted windows pulled up outside. The driver circled around until the car faced the exit drive.

"That's an Alpina B7 model," Rasco whispered. "They start at around a hundred and forty grand."

From this angle and with the dark windows, it was impossible for me to tell who was in the car. A moment later, Rasco pushed the rolling staircase in my direction. He'd laid his tablet on one of the steps with the information displayed. Per the search, the vehicle belonged to a man named Amit Venkatesh.

As I watched, a thin, brown-skinned man in his late thirties exited the vehicle, giving me a brief view of a black-haired woman in the passenger seat. Venkatesh had a neatly trimmed beard and was dressed in stylish business attire and a pair of mirrored sunglasses. His head turned as he looked around. Though he glanced briefly into our hangar, he apparently failed to identify me and Rasco as a threat. Our disguise had worked.

He stepped up to the door of hangar 38 and knocked. A moment later one of the men we'd seen earlier opened the door. Venkatesh disappeared inside.

I grabbed a rag and made my way over to the plane, standing on the steps and rubbing the cloth over the windows.

Climbing into the plane and taking a seat on the nearest row, Rasco placed his tablet on the fold-down table and continued his search. Not long afterward, he summoned me into the plane to share the results. I slid into the seat next to him.

44   DIANE KELLY

"Venkatesh is Indian," he said. "A jeweler. He owns stores in Mumbai and Dallas."

Hmm. Venkatesh's purchase of the gold could be for entirely aboveboard purposes. Then again, the jeweler surely had to question the source of the gold. Legitimate gold dealers didn't fly their gold in on private jets and hide it in suitcases. Rasco and I climbed back out of the plane. While I used the broom to remove cobwebs from the ceiling, my partner returned to the toolbox where he had a vantage point on the BMW. In a few minutes the door to hangar 38 opened. Venkatesh stepped out. He held his key fob in one hand and rolled a black suitcase with the other. The bag was large enough to hold dozens of standard 10-ounce bars. With the current price of gold averaging $1,900 an ounce, a full suitcase would be worth hundreds of thousands of dollars.

The man rested the suitcase on his back bumper while activating the car's trunk release on his key fob. The trunk popped open, revealing a matched set of Gucci luggage. As we spied through the doorway, Venkatesh fooled around with things in his trunk. Though we couldn't see exactly what he was doing, he appeared to be rearranging items in his bags and stowing the gold in the bottom of the largest suitcase.

"You think he's flying out of the country?" I whispered to Rasco.

"Good chance of it."

Though it was not illegal to take gold out of the country, anyone leaving with quantities valued at $2,500 or more was required to file a disclosure. Given the shady manner in which Venkatesh had obtained the gold and the high tariffs for gold imports into India, I doubted he'd comply with the reporting requirements.

The instant the BMW drove away, I phoned ICE agents at the airport. "Keep an eye out for Venkatesh and his bags."

In case the man's destination was somewhere other than the terminal, Rasco and I jumped into his Charger to follow

FIVE GOLD-SMUGGLING RINGS   45

the car. We drove out of our space and circled around hangar 36, hanging back so Venkatesh wouldn't realize he had a tail.

A few minutes later, the BMW turned into the long-term parking garage. We pulled into the lot, too, passing the BMW as it took a spot on the second level.

Rasco turned into a spot on the third tier and we quickly shed our jumpsuits. As Rasco tossed his ball cap into the back seat, I pulled the elastic from my pony tail. I fluffed my hair, noting Javier cast a glance my way. Was that lust gleaming in his eyes, or merely excitement from the pending bust?

Dressed inconspicuously now in jeans and long-sleeved tees, we made our way into the airport, heading to the international terminal.

"There he is." Javier cut his eyes to the check-in counter for British Airways.

Venkatesh and his female passenger stood at the desk, speaking with the clerk. Rasco and I held back, secreting ourselves behind a line of people waiting at security. We watched Venkatesh and the woman proceed to the customs counter. Venkatesh obtained what was presumably a customs declaration form from the male agent. The woman retrieved a pen from her Prada purse and handed it to him. When he'd completed the form, he handed it back to the agent.

Javier's eyes narrowed. "The moment of truth."

My skin tingled with anticipation.

The agent read the form over, said something to Venkatesh, then gestured for him to put his luggage on a nearby table. Though we could not hear what Venkatesh said in reply, it was clear from his gestures and expression he was attempting to negotiate with the agent. Never a good idea. It only made agents suspicious.

A second male agent stepped over, lifted the suitcases onto the table, and began to rummage around inside. He pulled the contents from the bags, placing them in a plastic bin. When the luggage was empty, he patted the bottom.

46   DIANE KELLY

Venkatesh and the woman began to back away, but their progress was halted by armed agents. As we watched, the agent searching the baggage used a box cutter to slice through the lining of the bag. A moment later he held up a bar of gold.

Busted.

Our work here was done.

I turned to Javier. "One suitcase down, four to go."

CHAPTER 8
TAKING OUT THE TRASH

Rasco and I returned to the car, slipped into our coveralls once again, and drove back to the hangar to resume our surveillance. Our efforts were rewarded just before noon when a silver Lincoln MKZ with New York license plates pulled up to the door. Three men sat inside. All had salt-and-pepper hair and wore callous expressions, like a trio of middle-aged Grinches.

Rasco retrieved his tablet and stood close to the inside wall, where he couldn't be seen from the outside. While he ran the license plate, I pretended to jot notes in the mainte-nance log and kept what I hoped was a discreet eye on the car. Not so easy to do when the man in the passenger seat seemed to be watching me in return as he devoured an enor-mous meatball sub. Did he suspect I wasn't actually a mainte-nance worker? I hoped not. The last thing we needed was for this bust to go bust.

The driver, a stocky man wearing an expensive business suit, stepped up to the door of hangar 38 and rapped on it with his meaty knuckles. Seconds later the door swung open and the man stepped into the hangar.

Rasco kept his voice low as he relayed information to me.

"The Lincoln belongs to a Joseph Campisi. He's got links to organized crime. Spent four years in the federal pen for extortion and money laundering."

"Looks like he hasn't changed his ways." No doubt the gold would be used in some off-balance-sheet financing.

Rasco tapped the screen. "Uh-oh. Says here he's wanted for questioning in connection with an execution-style murder in Brooklyn."

That was a pretty big *uh-oh.*

I closed the side door of the hangar. "Get back in the car," I told Rasco.

A grin tugged at his upper lip. "Thus, she takes charge."

"Was there any doubt I would?"

"None whatsoever."

Rasco drove out of the hangar and down the edge of the tarmac, staying out of sight of the mean-faced men. We exited the gate and waited outside the fence, concealed by a row of oleander bushes. While we waited, I put in a call to local police. Until officers could respond, I remained on the line with dispatch.

The Lincoln pulled out of the gate a few minutes later.

"They're on the move," I told the dispatcher.

"Four cruisers are en route," she replied.

We followed the car east on Airport Freeway until it exited onto Beltline Road and headed north. After a few turns on surface streets, a patrol car from Irving PD caught up with us.

"Two of the other cruisers are driving up parallel streets," the dispatcher informed me. "The fourth moved ahead to block the street in case the men attempt an escape."

The criminals were surrounded. *Good.*

Rasco pulled aside to let the cruiser pass. The officer at the wheel raised a hand in acknowledgment, then activated his lights and sirens. With a blaze of flashing lights and a *woo-woo-woo*, the car sped after the Lincoln. We followed on the cruiser's tail.

FIVE GOLD-SMUGGLING RINGS   49

When Campisi realized a cop was after him, he floored the gas pedal. Unfortunately for him, the cops had placed a spike strip on the road ahead. The Lincoln sped over the strip, only to slow to a bumpy crawl as all four tires lost air.

Rasco grunted. "Dumb ass. He ought to watch the road more carefully."

While the man in the backseat of the Lincoln raised his hands in surrender, Campisi and the man in the passenger seat leaped from the moving car and took off running in opposite directions. The car rolled into the back of another vehicle waiting at a red light and came to a stop. Ahead of us, the cop threw his cruiser into park, whipped out his gun, and ran toward the Lincoln.

"Campisi and a passenger bailed out," I told the dispatcher. "They're fleeing on foot." I gave her a quick description of the men so the officers on the adjacent streets could identify them. Of course, the fact that they were running for their lives would be a big clue.

The man in the back seat emerged from the car with his hands in the air. "Don't shoot!" He fell to his knees on the asphalt, apparently no stranger to arrest procedures.

Javier and I jumped from the Charger, Glocks in hand. Javier ran after Campisi, while I took off after the passenger.

As I ran past the police cruiser on the next street, I motioned and yelled, "This way!"

The cruiser fell in behind me as I pursued my quarry.

The mobster glanced back when he heard my footsteps pounding the asphalt, gaining on him. He'd have made better time if he'd cut back on the meatball subs.

"Stop!" I shouted.

He didn't stop, though. Instead, he kept right on running, through the parking lot of a hair salon and into a neighborhood park, tripping over a plastic pail and falling onto his hands and knees in the sand at the bottom of the playground slide. A chubby, curly-haired toddler careened down the

50   DIANE KELLY

slide, his tiny feet hitting the man in the shoulder. The man flopped onto his side, the bewildered child landing on him, giving me time to catch up. Fearing the man might take the kid hostage, I grabbed the boy and plunked him down in the sand behind me. He stood and took off running toward his mother, wobbling and wailing like a banshee.

By this time, the officer who'd followed me arrived on the scene. "Police!" he called to the women and children nearby. "Clear the area!"

While frantic mothers rounded up their children and fled, I pointed my gun down at the man.

"Call . . . an . . . ambulance!" he gasped, clutching his chest as he struggled in the sand. "I'm having . . . a . . . heart attack!"

"You sure?" I nudged him with my toe. "Maybe it's just heartburn from that sandwich."

His eyes rolled back in his head and a stream of drool flowed from his mouth. Looked like he was telling the truth. I yanked my phone from my pocket and summoned medical assistance.

Fifteen minutes later, Javier and I reunited at the Charger. He was alone, no mean-faced gangster in tow. I glanced around but didn't see Campisi secured in any of the cruisers. *Had he gotten away? Or had he already been hauled off to the station for booking?*

"Did you get Campisi?" I asked.

"No. A garbage truck did."

"Oh." My mind formed a bloody image. "Ew."

Javier grimaced. "You're telling me."

CHAPTER 9
ACTS OF CONGRESS

As we climbed into the car, my stomach growled.

"Hungry?" Rasco asked.

"Starving."

"What sounds good for lunch?"

"Anything but a meatball sub."

We drove through a burger stand, eating our lunch on the way back to the hangar. We pulled onto the main throughway just in time to see a grayish-blue Infiniti edge away from the back of hangar 38. Rasco turned left and circled around until the Charger was in place behind the car.

While Rasco drove, I retrieved my tablet and ran a search on the plate. "Does the name Stephen Galecki mean anything to you?"

Rasco shook his head. "No. You?"

"Nope."

An Internet search yielded several links. I clicked on the first one. "Says here he's chief of staff for Senator Dominic Stanko."

Javier's brows rose. "No shit?"

"No excrement whatsoever."

"This day just keeps getting more interesting."

Dominic Stanko, a former executive in the shipping industry, had been a U.S. senator for nearly two decades. During that time, he'd chalked up a questionable ethics record, accused of misusing campaign funds, selling votes, and boinking several wide-eyed college interns. The guy had more charisma than character, and managed to repeatedly convince others their suspicions were mislaid. Add that to the fact that he never did his own dirty work and it was impossible for authorities to pin anything on him. Time after time he skated by, as if he were a shaggy-haired adolescent boy in skinny jeans.

Was he accepting a bribe from Kayembe? Or was something else going on here?

We followed Galecki's sedan to a house in Keller, a smaller, upscale city in the outer metroplex. The car pulled into the driveway and a clean-cut, sandy-haired man in his forties emerged. He wore navy pants, a starched white dress shirt, and a red and white striped tie. He walked around to the passenger side, retrieving the suitcase from the floorboard. When he turned around, Javier and I were on him like white on rice.

"Stephen Galecki?" I asked.

His eyes narrowed. "Who wants to know?"

"Agent Dietrich." I flashed my badge. "Immigration and Customs Enforcement."

Rasco likewise flashed his badge and identified himself.

Galecki's gaze roamed over us, taking in our coveralls. "You don't look like ICE agents."

"And you don't look like a gold smuggler," I spat back. "But we all know that suitcase you're holding is loaded with ten-ounce bars."

"No, it's . . ." He stopped short of lying and looked away.

"Look," I said. "Senator Stanko has skated so far, but you and I both know his luck will run out sometime. When it does, he won't go down alone." I paused to give Galecki a moment to consider my words. "Whose house is this?" I used my chin to indicate the two-story gray brick residence in front of us. "Yours? Senator Stanko's?"

He turned blazing eyes on me. "You want answers? Get a subpoena." He turned to head inside only to find Rasco standing in his way.

Rasco had used his phone to run a search. "This house belongs to a Roslyn Galecki. She's your mother, isn't she?"

Galecki's jaw flexed. "Move. You have no authority to arrest me. Possession of gold isn't illegal."

"That's true," Rasco said. "And let me guess who told you that. Senator Stanko?"

Alarm flashed in Galecki's eyes, but he remained mum.

"Possession of gold may not be against the law," I said, "but you're aiding and abetting a crime. You know good and well the gold is either an illegal gift to the senator, a bribe, or that Senator Stanko will use the gold for some unlawful purpose. You want to go down with him? Or, worse yet, *for* him? Clearly, he's taken pains to keep his own nose clean. He's got you doing his dirty work. You're the one who will pay." Quite a persuasive speech, if I do say so myself.

Galecki's face became pensive as he appeared to debate his strategy for dealing with the two stubborn agents accosting him. Should he cooperate and rat out his boss? Or should he keep his mouth shut and let things play out? Apparently deciding that saying nothing posed the least amount of risk, Galecki stepped around Rasco and headed up the steps to the porch.

Rasco punched a button on his phone and put it to his ear. "Hello, Mrs. Galecki? Come to the front door, please. Your son is on your stoop and he has his hands full."

Galecki's head whipped around. "Don't you dare drag my mother into this!"

"Sorry, Stephen." I held up my hands to indicate the house. "You already have."

The door opened and an elderly woman looked out. "Why, hello there, honey!" she said to her son. "This is a nice surprise."

No, it wasn't. Not at all.

Her gaze went from her son to me and Rasco. "Are these two friends of yours?"

Again, not at all.

After Rasco told Mrs. Galecki the reason for our visit, she grabbed her son by the ear and pulled him and the suitcase into the foyer. "I told you Dom Stanko was a no-good liar. Now look at the mess you're in!"

She turned to me and Rasco. "Come inside. Let's talk things over."

A half hour later, the four of us were seated around Mrs. Galecki's living room. Stephen had been reduced to tears and offered his cooperation in nailing Senator Stanko, while I'd been reduced to a gelatinous mass after eating five of Mrs. Galecki's delicious home-baked, snowman-shaped frosted sugar cookies.

"Can I have your recipe?" I asked as we made our way back out the door.

She smiled and wagged a finger. "Nuh-uh-uh. It's a family secret."

I debated pistol-whipping her for a list of ingredients, but decided it wasn't worth the repercussions.

Rasco and I returned to the Charger with a signed affidavit from Stephen, the suitcase of gold as evidence, and a plastic zip-top bag full of cookies. All in all, not a bad day.

CHAPTER 10
ZAPPED

When we arrived back at the hangar late Thursday afternoon, the Taurus was gone. Looked like the two remaining gold deliveries would take place tomorrow. Good thing. After chasing down Campisi's cohort and indulging in the Christmas cookies, I was ready for a nap.

Our job done for the day, Javier and I locked up the hangar and headed back in the direction of the ICE office.

"Do you have dinner plans?" Javier asked.

"There's a burrito in my freezer that expires at midnight."

His lip quirked in disgust. "Leave the burrito in the freezer. Let's get some fresh Mexican food."

A thrill ran through me, but I did my best to hide it, feigning a nonchalant shrug. "Why not?"

He continued driving for a couple more miles, then exited the freeway and pulled into a strip center that housed a mom-and-pop Mexican restaurant with colorful piñatas hanging from the ceiling.

"It might not look like much," Javier said, "but hold your judgment until you've tried their guacamole."

We stepped inside and the hostess seated us at one of the

six tables, under a donkey-shaped piñata. Javier was right. The minute the seasoned guac hit my taste buds I thought I'd died and gone to heaven.

The two of us made small talk over dinner, surprised to find we had quite a bit in common. He, too, had excelled in track and field in high school, though his best events were the discus and high hurdles. He still ran three miles a day to stay in shape. Like me, he preferred watching Mavericks basketball over Cowboys football. He had a cat, too, sharing his condo with a calico named Cuddlekins.

Despite my best efforts, a snort escaped me. "Cuddlekins?"

"My sister forced the darn cat on me. She came with the name already attached." He showed me a dozen photos of the cat he'd taken on his phone, including one of Cuddlekins chewing the corner of a mystery novel and another with the cat hanging gleefully from a pair of shredded curtains. "She's terrible." The affection in his voice belied his words. He eyed me intently then, his tone changing from casual to more serious. "You know why I became an ICE agent. But I'm curious about you, Angelika. Why choose such a dangerous and demanding career?"

"Process of elimination. I'm not smart enough to cure cancer. I suck at math so engineering was out. And I'm not exactly built to be a figure skater."

His eyes narrowed. "Shoot straight with me."

I was flattered he wanted to get to know me, but dare I tell him the truth, which was corny and pitiful? One look in his brown eyes and I knew I could trust him. "When I was growing up, my parents and I watched spy movies together. Government agents always seemed smart and capable, and their work was intriguing. You know, undercover operations and secret identities and all that. I thought if I worked for the government I'd get to travel to exotic places and use fancy gadgets. I'm still waiting for that jet pack. I also thought ..." I stopped myself, unsure whether I was ready to share more. It was personal. Maybe *too* personal.

Javier tilted his head, a subtle sign of encouragement.

I took a breath and summoned my courage. "I thought it would be nice to be someone else sometimes, even if it was just pretending." Being me hadn't always been easy.

Javier stared at me for a moment before offering a soft smile. "Well, I, for one, am glad you're *you*."

I tried not to swoon in my seat.

Rasco insisted on paying for the meal, forcing my hand back when I pulled out my wallet. "My treat."

I didn't dare let myself consider the meal a date. It was nothing more than two coworkers sharing dinner after a busy day on the job, getting to know each other better. *Right?*

Sleep eluded me that night as my mind played over the events of the past two days. Javier's armor had not only been chinked, but had gaped wide open, giving me a glimpse of the man behind the badass façade. He was a tough, smart agent, no doubt about that. But that rugged exterior housed a sensitive side, too. He was clearly close to his mother and sister, and any man who would put up with such an annoying cat had to have both patience and a compassionate heart. Catching Guerra and putting him behind bars seemed to have lifted a huge weight from Javier, unburdened his soul, leaving him free now to enjoy life unfettered by grief and his thirst for vengeance. He was like Ebenezer Scrooge in *A Christmas Carol*, enjoying a new lease on life.

Still, I'd be a fool to think he considered me anything more than a companionable coworker. Why set myself up for heartache? Instead, I decided to make a New Year's resolution to find a boyfriend in time to celebrate Valentine's Day right. Maybe I'd sign up for one of those speed-dating events or join a singles group.

Early Friday morning, Rasco and I met at the office. The sky was gray and cloudy, and a brisk wind battered the car, the reprieve from winter weather over. Mother Nature was a fickle bitch. Good thing I'd brought myself an insulated travel mug full of hazelnut-flavored coffee. I'd brought a second travel mug for Javier.

"Here you go." I held it out to him.

"What is it?"

"Hazelnut coffee." I knew he'd like it. I'd noticed he kept a container of flavored creamer in the break room refrigerator. Heck, I'd stolen a dash or two on occasion, hoping he wouldn't notice.

He took the mug from me and unscrewed the top, releasing the delicious aroma. Taking a sip, he closed his eyes in caffeinated bliss. I might buy store-brand cereal, but I forked over the big bucks when it came to coffee. *Priorities.*

"None of my partners has brought me coffee before. Of course, they were all men." He took another, bigger sip and cut a look my way. "Maybe I should ask to be paired up with a female agent more often."

We arrived at the hangar to find it still closed up from the night before. Javier hopped out to enter the code, and the wide main door slid open. I drove the Charger into the hangar while my partner followed on foot, closing the door behind us to keep out the bristling arctic air.

My breath came in steamy puffs as I climbed out of the car. Even with my heavy jacket and knit cap I feared I'd freeze to death. We Texans could handle summer temperatures over 100 degrees for days at a time, but if the mercury dipped below 32 we turned into a bunch of shivering wimps.

"Look what I found." Javier pulled a space heater out of a storage closet.

I raised my hands in the air. "Hallelujah!"

The device would be incapable of warming the cavernous space, but if we sat directly in front of it we had a chance of avoiding frostbite.

Javier plugged the heater in near the door and pushed the

rolling staircase over in front of it for us to sit on. While I settled on the stairs with my steaming coffee, he retrieved a duffel bag from the trunk of his car. He set the bag on the floor, unzipped it, and pulled out a roll of see-through window film and a small box cutter.

"What are you doing?" I asked.

"You'll see."

As I watched, he applied the film to the square window in the hangar's side door and used the blade to trim the excess. While those looking in would see only a reflective lining in the window, Rasco and I would be able to look out through the window undetected.

I raised my mug in salute. "That's thinking ahead."

"You do enough of these stakeouts," he said, "you learn a few tricks."

At least we wouldn't have to pretend to be working in the hangar today. Instead, we could play games and watch videos on our tablets until there was some action at hangar 38.

Finished, Rasco took a seat on the step below me, close enough for me to smell the fresh scent of his shampoo and spy a tiny, adorable freckle on the nape of his neck that just begged to be kissed.

After an hour playing games on our phones to pass the time, we caught some action outside. The Taurus had returned. The same two men from the day before climbed out and entered the adjacent hangar, closing the door behind them.

A few minutes later, while I was distracted with online Christmas shopping, Rasco nudged my leg with his elbow and pointed out the window. "We've got company."

Outside, a white panel van pulled up between the hangars. On the side of the truck was a logo for Cheep PCs, Inc., a local company that produced inexpensive, off-brand computers. Their logo featured a cartoon laptop with a squawking canary on the screen, the word *Cheep!* hovering over the bird in a conversation bubble. The driver climbed down from the van and knocked on the door to Kayembe's hangar.

"What would an electronics company want with gold?" Rasco asked.

Now it was my turn to teach him something. "Gold is a good conductor," I replied. "There's a tiny bit of it in virtually every electronic device from cell phones to GPS systems to computers."

"Huh," he said. "You learn something new every day."

True. I'd learned this information only two days before, when researching gold online. As I'd also learned, per rules adopted by the Securities and Exchange Commission, companies purchasing conflict gold were required to file a public report on Form SD, which stood for Specialized Disclosure. Unfortunately, while the companies were required to divulge their purchases of the conflict gold, it was not illegal for them to buy the gold. I shared this information with Javier.

"The hope is that manufacturers will be shamed into doing the right thing," I added.

"You've done your homework, I see." Javier descended to the floor of the hangar and held his tablet up to the window, snapping photos of the Cheep PC employee carrying the suitcase of gold to the van. Meanwhile, I logged on to my tablet and pulled up the SEC filings. As expected, no Form SD had been filed by Cheep PC.

Rasco and I hopped into the Charger and followed our prey. As we headed west on Highway 183, I phoned the local SEC enforcement office, which had jurisdiction over the matter. When the receptionist transferred me to an available agent, I gave her the rundown.

"Conflict gold?" she said. "Appalling."

Consumers might like inexpensive electronics, but they weren't heartless. The fact that Cheep PC had not only bought conflict gold but also failed to report it wouldn't sit well with

FIVE GOLD-SMUGGLING RINGS 61

the public. Once the news hit the airwaves, Cheep PC would be out of business and its greedy owners would face stiff fines.

I attached the photographs to an e-mail. "The evidence is on its way."

The van merged onto the loop, then took the exit for US-377 south into Haltom City. Minutes later, the driver pulled up to a gate at Cheep PC's manufacturing facility. Just as the van entered the facility's secure compound, the SEC agent pulled up in her car and gave us a wave, letting us know she'd take things from here.

Javier executed a U-turn. "This was too easy. I was hoping to crack some skulls."

"Maybe Santa will put a skull in your stocking. Have you been a good boy this year?"

He slid a dark, dangerous grin my way. "Not at all."

CHAPTER 11
THREE TIMES THE FUN

After a quick stop for donuts to enjoy with our coffee, Rasco and I made our way back to the airport. Before pulling into our space, we noticed that the main door to Kayembe's hangar stood open now. The pilot and copilot moved about inside, preparing the plane for departure. Time was running out.

At eleven thirty, the rumble of a truck engine drew our attention to the window. I stepped to the glass for a closer look.

Outside, a Dodge Ram pickup pulled to a stop. The truck was burnt orange with a mega cab, the pricey Laramie Longhorn model. A magnetic sign on the door read HARRINGTON OIL & GAS. A tall, trim fiftyish man in snakeskin boots, creased blue jeans, and a western shirt climbed down from the cab, his straw Stetson in his hand. His auburn hair and thick red mustache were unmistakable.

"Holy crap!" I cried. "That's Hank Harrington."

"He some kind of big shot?" Having lived in the Dallas area only a short time, Javier apparently had yet to hear of the man.

"Harrington's a local billionaire and philanthropist," I

explained. "He and his wife are always doing some charity event or another. He's got more money than God."

Harrington had funded buildings at several area colleges and contributed priceless pieces to art museums. He was a local icon, the son of a roughneck who worked the oil rigs in west Texas. Garnering a scholarship to Harvard Business School, he'd overcome his poor roots, made some wise and lucky investments, and earned such big returns that he was able to buy the company his father had worked for.

But this larger-than-life man was not without detractors. His employees claimed he treated them like slaves, and his grown children alleged he'd been an absentee father with little interest in his family. With his money had come power, and the power had gone to his head. But buying conflict gold? That was a new low, even for a ruthless businessman like him.

Javier stepped up so close behind me I could feel his body heat. The additional warmth was welcome given the frigid temps today. Heck, I'd welcome Javier's body heat in the middle of a hellacious Texas summer.

We watched as Harrington raised a fist and pounded on the door of hangar 38. A moment later, the Congolese men appeared at the door. The one carrying the suitcase held it out to Harrington, but instead of taking it Harrington pointed at his truck, obviously expecting the other man to do the heavy lifting. Seemed the tycoon considered himself to be above menial labor. *What an ego.*

Harrington stepped over to his truck with Jean Paul and Rodrigue following. When Harrington opened the back door, the man carrying the bag slid it into the backseat. Just as Harrington closed the door, a taxi pulled up. Nicia sat in the back, walled in by her bodyguards. An older man, presumably her father, sat in the front passenger seat.

"We've gotta move now," Javier said over my shoulder, "or we'll lose the pilot and copilot."

64   DIANE KELLY

While Kayembe enjoyed diplomatic immunity, the privilege did not extend to his service staff. Jean Paul and Rodrigue were fair game. But we had to arrest them now, while they were on U.S. soil. Once the plane took off, they'd be home free.

A fellow agent had agreed to be on call should we need one of the agency's SUVs to transport detainees to the detention facility. I placed a quick call to the agent. "Come now with the transport."

Badges in hand and weapons at the ready, Rasco and I burst out the hangar door.

"Federal agents!" I shouted. "Hands up!"

After a panicked glance in our direction, both the pilot and copilot took off running. They got only a half dozen steps before Rasco tackled one of them to the asphalt. While I cuffed the man, Rasco leveraged himself to a stand and took off after the other, who now had a fifty-yard lead down the tarmac. Harrington merely crossed his arms over his chest and leaned back against his truck, his expression impassive. *Damn.* I'd hoped to scare the guy, at least a little.

Kayembe and the bodyguards leaped from the taxi and stormed toward me.

"What's going on here?" Kayembe shouted in accented English.

"We're agents with Customs Enforcement," I explained. "We caught your men transferring gold that wasn't declared when you entered the country."

Kayembe exchanged glances with his bodyguards. A forced smile spread his lips when he turned back to me. "This is merely a minor oversight. If you will provide me the proper form, I would be happy to complete it."

Too late, buddy. "The gold has been transferred to an Indian smuggler, a congressman, and members of organized crime, among others. Moreover, we suspect it's conflict gold. I'd hardly call this a minor oversight."

FIVE GOLD-SMUGGLING RINGS   65

When Nicia began to climb out of the cab, her father gestured for her to remain in the car. He said something to his bodyguards under his breath in French.

Harrington dropped his arms and turned toward his truck, reaching for the door handle. "Y'all got nothin' on me."

I stepped in front of the man. "You're not going anywhere yet. We've got some questions for you."

Harrington grunted. "I'm not talking until I've got an attorney present."

"Well, then," I said, "give your attorney a call."

Chances were, we'd get nothing useful out of the man and have to release him, but that wasn't going to stop me from giving him a little hell first. The man was involved in shady business and deserved some inconvenience to go with his legal bills. Some poor, oppressed Africans might mean nothing to him, but the loss of time and money would make him think twice.

A roar sounded to my right. I looked through the side door to Kayembe's hangar to see the plane roll forward. The pilot must have circled back to the hangar and climbed inside.

Rasco stood in front of the plane, his palms raised. "Stop!"

The pilot ignored him, continuing forward until Rasco was forced to jump aside or be run over.

Time for some quick thinking. How the hell could I stop a plane? I wasn't exactly King Kong.

But I do have some shapeless coveralls I no longer need.

Zzzzzip! I yanked the zipper down and stepped out of the jumpsuit. Scooping up the uniform I ran to the main door of Kayembe's hangar just as the plane raced out of it. Mustering all my strength, I hurled my coveralls into the engine on my side. There was a burst of flame as the engine consumed the fabric, then fell silent. The other engine, however, continued to roar.

Following my lead, Rasco ripped a shoe from his foot, ran after the plane, and hurled it into the other engine. A spurt of flame erupted from that engine, too, before the pilot cut the power and rolled to a stop on the tarmac, evidently deciding surrender was preferable to the near-certain death he'd suffer if he tried to take the damaged aircraft into the air.

Javier turned to me, his lips curved up in a smile. "Quick thinking, Angelika!"

I shrugged though, honestly, I was impressed with myself, too.

Twenty minutes later, our fellow ICE agent arrived with the transport vehicle and we loaded Jean Paul, Rodrigue, and Harrington into the back.

"My attorney will make fools of you!" Harrington barked before we closed the door on him.

What an asshole.

Kayembe and the bodyguards climbed back into the taxi, where Kayembe ordered the driver to follow the transport vehicle. Kayembe whipped out his cell phone, presumably to call lawyers and see who might be available on short notice. Nicia glanced out the window, offering me a conspiratorial wink. I offered her one in return.

Our work at the airport done, Rasco and I drove his Charger to the detention facility in Seagoville, where Harrington and Kayembe's pilot and copilot had been taken. On the advice of legal counsel, all three refused to speak with us, pleading their Fifth Amendment right against self-incrimination. No bother, really. We had enough circumstantial evidence to nail the pilot and copilot, and Harrington would be tried in the local press. Once the *Dallas Morning News* got wind of his sleazy dealings and issued a condemning exposé, he'd be persona non grata in social and business circles. No doubt his wife would continue her charitable endeavors in order to save face.

Rasco and I returned to the office just after four o'clock. Beldaccio caught us on his way out.

He raised his hand for a high five. "Nice work the last few days, Dietrich."

I slapped his hand. "Does this mean I can ditch Granny? Maybe trade her for the blue Malibu?"

"What the hell," my boss said. "It's Christmas."

CHAPTER 12
VISIONS OF SUGARPLUMS

After the excitement of the past three days, spending Friday evening at home alone was anticlimactic. All of my friends had dates or holiday parties to attend. I ended up curled up on the couch with Mister Mow-Mow, watching *It's a Wonderful Life* and sharing the frozen burrito.

The rest of the weekend was marginally better. On Saturday, I wrapped up my holiday shopping, even found a cute red and white striped sweater, perfect for next week's holiday office party. On Sunday, I attended the children's choir program at the church, where my nephew sang Christmas carols. Still, spending the holidays without someone special was a little depressing.

Back at work on Monday, the toilets flushed, the supply cabinet door rattled, and Javier was nowhere to be seen. I was dying to find out if his mother had received her shoes and what she'd thought of them. Oh, who was I kidding? I was dying to see the guy again. Working with him last week had been wonderful. If anything, my silly crush had only grown crushier, if there was such a word.

But that wasn't exactly true, was it? My infatuation had

FIVE GOLD-SMUGGLING RINGS   69

evolved over the short but concentrated time Javier and I had spent together. My feelings had become a real attraction to the man I'd come to know. I'd learned what made him tick, that he had a vulnerable side, that the man I'd once thought of as cold and heartless was in fact just the opposite.

When Rasco's space was still dark that afternoon, I ventured toward Beldaccio's office. I tried to sound casual as I addressed his secretary. "Hey, Nancy. I haven't seen Agent Carrasco around today. Is he out on assignment?"

She stacked files on her desk. "He called this morning to say he'd flown back to Tucson."

"Any idea when he'll be back?"

She raised her palms. "Who knows? The guy had sixty days' accrued vacation."

My heart skipped a beat when I realized he might never come back. After all, his reason for transferring to Dallas no longer existed. Guerra was behind bars. Having accomplished his aims, would Rasco return to Tucson? After all, he had family there, roots, maybe even a girlfriend for all I knew.

The week dragged by. I assisted in an investigation regarding bootleg DVDs and, in the evenings, watched the children's Christmas specials on television. *Rudolph the Red-Nosed Reindeer. The Year Without a Santa Claus. The Little Drummer Boy.* But those *pa-rum-pum-pum-pums* only made me heartsick. To cheer myself up I attempted to make a gingerbread house, but the frosting wasn't thick enough and the whole thing collapsed in on itself. All it needed now was a CONDEMNED sign. So much for my holiday spirit.

After work on Friday, my coworkers and I gathered at the Ginger Man for the office party. Though I'd looked forward to the gathering before, all I really wanted to do now was curl up on my couch with a mug of hot chocolate laced with three fingers of rum-pum-pum-pum. But I couldn't poop on my own party, right?

I played my role as a jolly-old elf the best I could, smiling

70   DIANE KELLY

warmly and shaking the Christmas bell on the red cord around my neck as each person arrived. In minutes, the holiday spirit overtook me, thanks to two rounds of a sugar-rimmed drink called a candy cane, which contained a generous portion of peppermint schnapps.

After an hour of holiday-related chit-chat, we proceeded with the white elephant gift exchange. Each gift was worse than the one before. A silly souvenir snow globe from Hawaii, featuring palm trees and hula dancers. A poorly rendered velvet painting of a sunflower. A Darth Vader nutcracker.

Nancy reached into a shiny green gift bag and pulled out a cookbook. *"101 Beet-tastic Recipes?"* Her nose scrunched in disgust.

Beldaccio's gift was a yellow knit cap with black fuzz sticking up on top in a simulated mohawk.

"Dude!" one of my male coworkers called from down the table. "You look totally rad!"

The last to open my gift, I tore into a box wrapped in Santa-print paper to find a tacky red birdhouse trimmed with sparkly beads. "Is this a bird*house* or a bird *brothel*?"

As we laughed at the tacky gift, a shadow fell over the table. I glanced up to find Rasco standing behind me.

"Sorry I'm late." He grabbed a chair from a nearby table and squeezed in beside me. "Our flight was delayed by bad weather over New Mexico."

I was so glad to see the guy I had to fight not to throw my arms around him.

Wait. Did he say *our*? Who had flown back with him? A girlfriend?

Nancy—*God bless her!*—asked the question on my tongue. "Who came with you?"

"My mother and sister," Javier said. "They've never been to Dallas so I invited them to celebrate Christmas at my place."

Relief flowed through me.

FIVE GOLD-SMUGGLING RINGS 71

Rasco placed a small wrapped gift on the table and signaled the waiter for a beer.

"We've already finished the gift exchange," I told him.

"That's okay." He pushed the box toward me. "This is for you. From my mother."

My gaze met his for a moment and my throat swelled with emotion. Obviously, he had told his mother about me, about the role I played in putting an end to Guerra's life of crime, in finally giving the family some closure. I opened the box to find a holiday tin filled with small grainy squares.

"They're *dulce de alegría*," Rasco explained. "The Mexican answer to Rice Krispies treats."

"'Tis the season of sharing!" Nancy reached across the table to snatch a piece from the tin.

Before I knew what was happening, half of the squares had been snagged by my coworkers. But Nancy was right. The holidays were a time to share.

I bit into a piece and nearly fell over. The taste was both nutty and sweet. "This is delicious!"

Javier smiled. "My mother will be happy you liked them." He fished a piece out of the tin for himself. "The shoes were a big hit, by the way."

"Told you they would be."

He chuckled. "I'll never doubt you again."

An hour later, everyone had begged off, going home to family or to attend other holiday events. Everyone but Javier and me, that is.

"I guess we should go now, too." I stood from the table.

"I'll walk you to your truck."

Javier strode silently beside me as I made my way out of the pub, onto the sidewalk, and into the lot.

When we reached my truck, I bleeped my doors open and climbed inside. "See you back at work after Christmas."

When I reached for my door handle, he put a hand on the frame to stop me. "Are you busy New Year's Eve?"

My heart beat so loud I could hear it. *Pa-rum-pum-pum-pum!* "Whuh?"

A grin played about his mouth. "Caught you off guard?"

When I was able to speak again, I said, "Little bit."

He leaned in closer. "You seeing anyone, Angelika?"

Pum-pum-pum! "No."

"Me neither. It would be a shame for us to be alone on New Year's."

"I agree."

His let his lips spread in a grin. "I'll pick you up at seven."

PA-RUM-PUM-PUM-PUM!

CHAPTER 13
MIDNIGHT KISS

Christmas with my extended family was its usual mix of festivity, food, and chaos. I found myself wondering how Javier and his family were enjoying their Christmas, whether this might be my last Christmas alone.

On New Year's Eve, a knock sounded on the door to my apartment promptly at 7:00. Taking a breath to calm my nerves, I walked to the door and opened it.

Javier's gaze slid from my face, down over my new red dress, to my red-tipped toenails in my sparking stilettos. "Wow! You look ..." His head tilted as he seemed to search his brain for precise words. Apparently, he found none. "Wow!"

Wow would do just fine. No sense taxing the man's brain when he was so clearly stunned by my gorgeousness.

I looked Javier over. He wore a traditional black tux with a red bow tie and cummerbund, and looked absolutely edible. "You look pretty *wow* yourself."

He took me to dinner at the Old Warsaw, where we indulged in a delicious dinner paired with a nice cabernet, topped off with a Grand Marnier soufflé for dessert. I was so stuffed afterward I was afraid the seams would split on my dress.

We headed over to the Rattlesnake Bar. My friends wouldn't mind me bringing Javier along. Heck, I wanted to show him off. Besides, when I told him my single friends would be meeting up at the bar, he immediately texted three guys he shot hoops with at the gym. All it took were the words *single ladies* to convince them to join us.

His friends and mine hit it off, and soon we were all on the dance floor. Javier was as good a dancer as he was an agent, smooth with impeccable rhythm. As the evening progressed, the dance floor grew more crowded, forcing us closer. I didn't mind a bit. The smile on his face told me he didn't mind, either.

"Ten!" shouted the crowd as the countdown to midnight began. "Nine!"

Javier and I joined in, counting down until we were shouting, "Three! Two! One!"

Javier's gaze met mine and he gently cupped my chin with his hand. Closing his eyes, he leaned in and pressed his lips to mine, kissing me softly. His kiss was as sweet as the *dulce de alegría.*

No doubt about it. This was going to be a wonderful new year.

ABOUT THE AUTHOR

A former tax advisor, Diane Kelly inadvertently worked with white-collar criminals more than once. Lest she end up in an orange jumpsuit, Diane decided self-employment would be a good idea. Her fingers hit the keyboard and thus began her "Death and Taxes" romantic mystery series. A graduate of her hometown's Citizen Police Academy, Diane Kelly also writes the hilarious Paw Enforcement K-9 series, the Busted female motorcycle cop series, the House Flipper series, the Southern Homebrew moonshine series, and the Mountain Lodge Mysteries series.

Diane's books have been awarded the prestigious Romance Writers of America Golden Heart® Award and a Reviewers Choice Award.

Find Diane online at www.DianeKelly.com, on her Author Diane Kelly page on Facebook, and at @DianeKellyBooks on Instagram, Twitter/X, Pinterest, and TikTok. Be the first to receive book news by signing up for her newsletter at: https://www.dianekelly.com/newsletter/

facebook.com/DianeKellyBooks

twitter.com/DianeKellyBooks

instagram.com/dianekellybooks

ALSO BY DIANE KELLY

The Busted series:

Busted

Another Big Bust

Busting Out

The Mountain Lodge Mysteries:

Getaway With Murder

A Trip With Trouble

Snow Place for Murder

The Southern Homebrew series:

The Moonshine Shack Murder

The Proof is in the Poison

Fiddling With Fate

The House Flipper series:

Dead as a Door Knocker

Dead in the Doorway

Murder With a View

Batten Down the Belfry

Primer and Punishment

The Paw Enforcement series:

Paw Enforcement

Paw and Order

Upholding the Paw (a bonus novella)

Laying Down the Paw

Against the Paw

Above the Paw

Enforcing the Paw

The Long Paw of the Law

Paw of the Jungle

Bending the Paw

The Tara Holloway Death & Taxes series:

Death, Taxes, and a French Manicure

Death, Taxes, and a Skinny No-Whip Latte

Death, Taxes, and Extra-Hold Hairspray

Death, Taxes, and a Sequined Clutch (a bonus novella)

Death, Taxes, and Peach Sangria

Death, Taxes, and Hot Pink Leg Warmers

Death, Taxes, and Green Tea Ice Cream

Death, Taxes, and Mistletoe Mayhem (a bonus novella)

Death, Taxes, and Silver Spurs

Death, Taxes, and Cheap Sunglasses

Death, Taxes, and a Chocolate Cannoli

Death, Taxes, and a Satin Garter

Death, Taxes, and Sweet Potato Fries

Death, Taxes, and Pecan Pie (a bonus novella)

Death, Taxes, and a Shotgun Wedding

Other Mysteries and Romances:

The Trouble With Digging Too Deep

Almost an Angel

Five Gold Smuggling Rings

Love Unleashed

Love, Luck, & Little Green Men

One Magical Night

A Sappy Love Story

Manufactured by Amazon.ca
Acheson, AB